Down in the Woods at Sleepytime

Carole Lexa Schaefer illustrated by Vanessa Cabban

WALKER BOOKS
AND SUBSIDIARIES
LONDON • BOSTON • SYDNEY

Deep down in the woods,
Mama Bear says, "It's sleepytime."

"No, uh-uh," grumble her cubs.
"We still want to play."

And they clown around

in the scruffy brush.

Deep down in the woods,
Mama Hedgehog says, "It's sleepytime."

"No, uh-uh," squeal her prickly babies.
"We're still hungry."

And they snuffle for snacks

in the mossy grass.

Deep down in the woods,
Mama Rabbit says, "It's sleepytime."

"No, uh-uh," squeak her bunnies.
"We're still peek-a-booing."

And hip-hop, they hide

under fat green leaves.

Deep down in the woods,
Mama Toad says, "It's sleepytime."

"No, hmm-mmm," hum her toadlets.
"We're still making up songs."

And "Hmm goo, mmm blup,"

they sing from the top of their log.

Deep down in the woods,
on her branch above them all,
wise Grandma Owl hoots,

"Whoo-hoo!
It's storytime."

And she begins.

"Deep down in the woods, bear cubs are nestling, cosy in the leaves,

baby hedgehogs are curling into tight warm balls,

bunnies snuggle close to each other

and toadlets settle softly in the goo glup mud..."

Wise Grandma Owl
blinks her big eyes.
She looks around...

"Whoo-hoo," hoots wise Grandma Owl.

"Sweet

dreams."